TOWNSHIP OF WASHINGTON PUBLIC LIBRARY
3 9149 09126463 0
W9-AFC-305

PUP
DETECT

BATTLE OF THE BANDS

Written by FELIX GUMPAW
Illustrated by GLASS HOUSE GRAPHICS

LITTLE SIMON
NEW YORK LONDON TORONTO SYDNEY NEW DELHI

THIS BOOK IS A WORK OF FICTION. ANY REFERENCES TO HISTORICAL EVENTS, REAL PEOPLE, OR REAL PLACES ARE USED FICTITIOUSLY. OTHER NAMES, CHARACTERS, PLACES, AND EVENTS ARE PRODUCTS OF THE AUTHOR'S IMAGINATION, AND ANY RESEMBLANCE TO ACTUAL EVENTS OR PLACES OR PERSONS, LIVING OR DEAD, IS ENTIRELY COINCIDENTAL.

LITTLE SIMON
AN IMPRINT OF SIMON & SCHUSTER CHILDREN'S PUBLISHING DIVISION
1230 AVENUE OF THE AMERICAS, NEW YORK, NEW YORK 10020
FIRST LITTLE SIMON EDITION OCTOBER 2022

ART AND COLORS BY GLASS HOUSE GRAPHICS • LETTERING BY MARCOS MASSAO INOUE • SUPERVISION BY MJ MACEDO/STUPLENDO • ART SERVICES BY GLASS HOUSE GRAPHICS •

DESIGNED BY NICHOLAS SCIACCA
MANUFACTURED IN CHINA 0522 SCP
10 9 8 7 6 5 4 3 2 1
LIBRARY OF CONGRESS CATALOGING-IN-PUBLICATION DATA
NAMES: GUMPAW, FELIX, AUTHOR. I GLASS HOUSE GRAPHICS, ILLUSTRATOR.
TITLE: BATTLE OF THE BANDS / BY FELIX GUMPAW ; ILLUSTRATED BY GLASS HOUSE GRAPHICS.
DESCRIPTION: FIRST LITTLE SIMON EDITION. I NEW YORK : LITTLE SIMON, 2022. I SERIES: PUP DETECTIVES ; 8 I AUDIENCE: AGES 5–9. I AUDIENCE: GRADES K–1. I SUMMARY: "THE BATTLE OF THE BANDS IS OFF TO A HAUNTING START WHEN A GHOST TRIES TO SCARE MUSIC AWAY FROM PAWSTON FOREVER!"– PROVIDED BY PUBLISHER. IDENTIFIERS: LCCN 2021053981 (PRINT) I LCCN 2021053982 (EBOOK) I ISBN 9781665912228 (PB) I ISBN 9781665912235 (HC) I ISBN 9781665912242 (EBOOK) SUBJECTS: CYAC: GRAPHIC NOVELS. I MYSTERY AND DETECTIVE STORIES. I DOGS–FICTION. I ANIMALS–FICTION. I BANDS (MUSIC)–FICTION. I CONTESTS–FICTION. I LCGFT: GRAPHIC NOVELS. I DETECTIVE AND MYSTERY FICTION. CLASSIFICATION: LCC PZ7.7.G858 BAT 2022 (PRINT) I LCC PZ7.7.G858 (EBOOK) I DDC 741.5/973–DC23/ENG/20220309
LC RECORD AVAILABLE AT HTTPS://LCCN.LOC.GOV/2021053981
LC EBOOK RECORD AVAILABLE AT HTTPS://LCCN.LOC.GOV/2021053982

CONTENTS

CHAPTER 1
PAWSTON ELEMENTARY LIBRARY
WELCOME BACK TO PAWSTON ELEMENTARY.
A SCHOOL WHERE ANYTHING CAN HAPPEN AT ANY TIME.
The Sound and The Furry
SO A PUP DETECTIVE HAS TO ALWAYS STUDY WITH ONE EYE OPEN AND ONE EAR UP.

BUT IT HELPS TO HAVE MORE THAN ONE PUP DETECTIVE IN YOUR PACK.

THIS IS RORA. SHE ALWAYS LOOKS OUT FOR THE LITTLE GUY.

HEY.
WAIT YOUR TURN!

AND WHAT'S A PUP DETECTIVE PACK WITHOUT AN INVENTOR?
DO YOU WISH YOU HAD A BEST FRIEND WHO NEVER LEFT YOUR SIDE? THEN MEET BEST FRIEND FOREVER ROBOT!
MEET WESTIE.
HE'S ALWAYS READY TO LEND A HELPING PAW.
OFF
CLICK!
EVEN IF IT'S NOT ALWAYS SO HELPFUL.
How to build a better robot!
Small Rocket
Big Rocket
I'M SURE IT WILL COME BACK.

AND OF COURSE, A PUP DETECTIVE NEEDS A NOSE FOR MYSTERIES.

AND NO NOSE KNOWS MYSTERIES BETTER THAN ZIGGY'S NOSE.

SNIFF

SNIFF SNIFF

I SOLVED THE CASE OF WHAT SMELLS SOOOOO GOOD.

CAN I SNAG A NIBBLE OF THAT?

AND I THINK I JUST SNIFFED OUT OUR NEXT CASE.

I DID IT!
I'VE GOT THE
GOODS!

I KNEW
IT!

COOKIES? PENCILS? BOOKS?

BOOKS ABOUT PENCILS AND COOKIES?

NAH, DUDE. WE'RE GONNA STEAL...

THE SHOW!

HUH?

BATTLE OF THE BANDS
IT'S A BATTLE OF THE BANDS!
BATTLE OF THE BANDS
BATTLE OF THE BANDS
BATTLE OF THE BANDS
A BATTLE OF THE BANDS?
WAIT, WHAT?
YEAH, ALL OUR BANDS ARE PLAYING, SO WE EACH MADE POSTERS.

NOW WE HAVE TO DECIDE WHO MADE THE *BEST* POSTER TO HANG UP, SO KIDS KNOW ABOUT THE SHOW.
LIBRARY

I CAN HELP WITH THAT.

I HAVE AN EYE FOR CLUES.

AND AN EYE FOR COOL!
OH YEAHHHHH!!!

CHAPTER 2

A BATTLE OF THE BANDS AT PAWSTON?
AWESOME!
WAIT.
SINCE WHEN DOES RIDER HAVE AN EYE FOR COOL?

MY PATENTED ALL-TERRAIN DRUM SET!
WHOOSH!

ATD FOR SHORT!
WESTIE, I HAVE TO SAY...

...THIS HAS GOT TO BE YOUR WEIRDEST INVENTION YET!

WEIRDER THAN HIS TINY-MINI COMB-A-MATIC?
HOW ELSE WOULD FLEAS COMB THEIR HAIR?
OR YOUR SMELL-ER-RATOR.
THAT THING JUST MADE WEIRD SMELLS.
YEAH.
THAT ONE *DID* STINK.

WELL, IT CAN'T BE WEIRDER THAN MY SYRUP SOAKER UPPER.
HMMMMM.
YEAH, YOU'RE RIGHT.
THAT WAS JUST A BIG WAFFLE.
VERY WEIRD!
AND VERY DELICIOUS!

HEY, THIS ATD MAY BE VERY WEIRD, BUT IT'S ALSO VERY COOL.

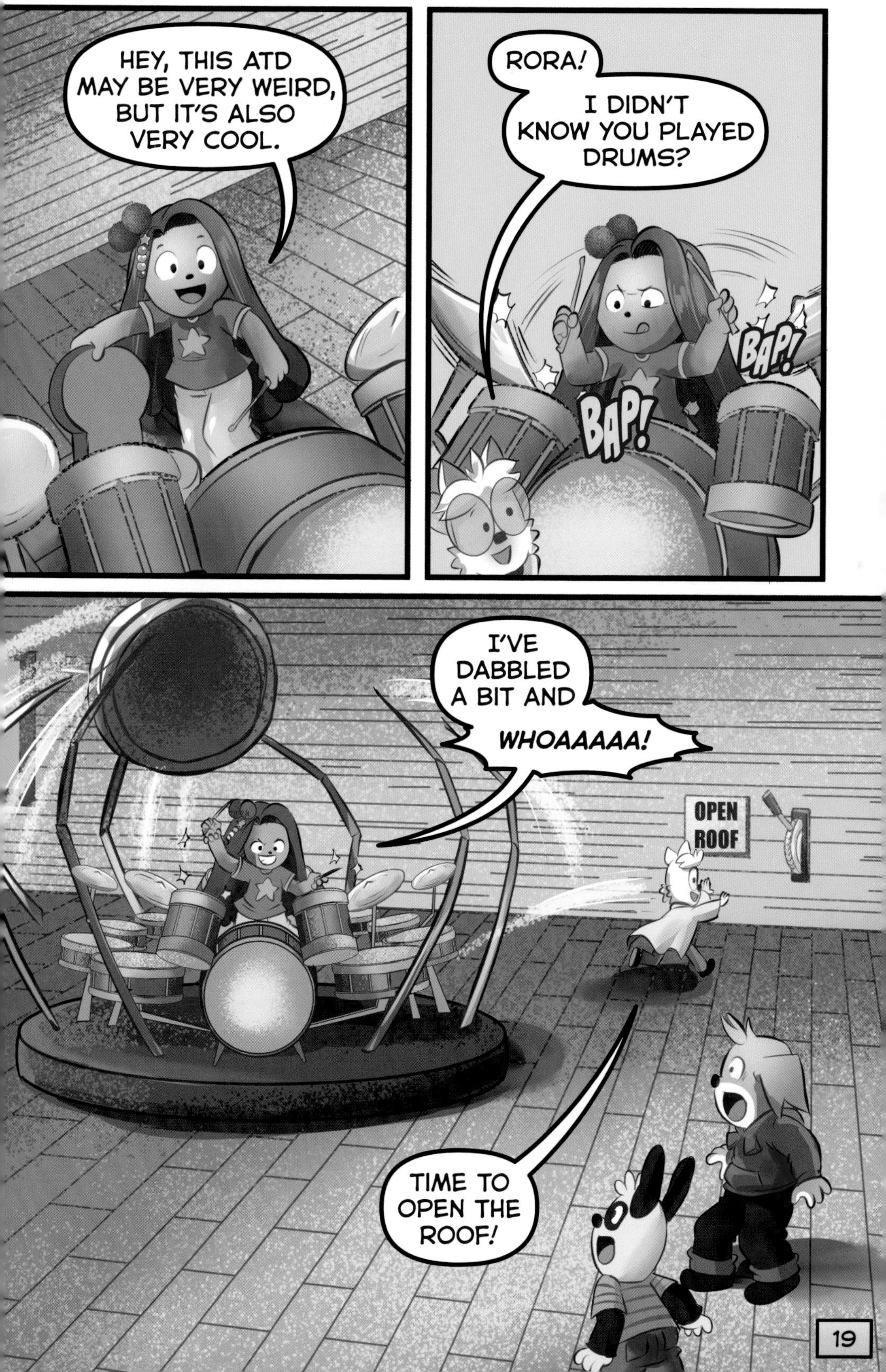

RORA!
I DIDN'T KNOW YOU PLAYED DRUMS?
BAP!
BAP!

I'VE DABBLED A BIT AND

WHOAAAAA!

OPEN ROOF

TIME TO OPEN THE ROOF!

BAKERY
PAWSTON MUSIC SHOP
The Band Zone Practice Spaces

PHEW. THAT WAS CLOSE.
CLICK!
WHOA.
NICE BEATS.
WHO DO YOU PLAY WITH?

OH, NO ONE. I'M A DETECTIVE, NOT A MUSICIAN.

YOU SHOULD JOIN OUR BAND!
YEAH, WE NEED A DRUMMER BAD!

I'M CAT BENATAR.
AND THIS IS CHEETAH FORD.
YEAH!
WE PLAY GUITAR!
I'M KIRA ROTTWEILER, AND I SLAP THE BASS.
BOOM BA BOOM
I'M THE SINGER! RUBY ROCKER! AND WE ARE...

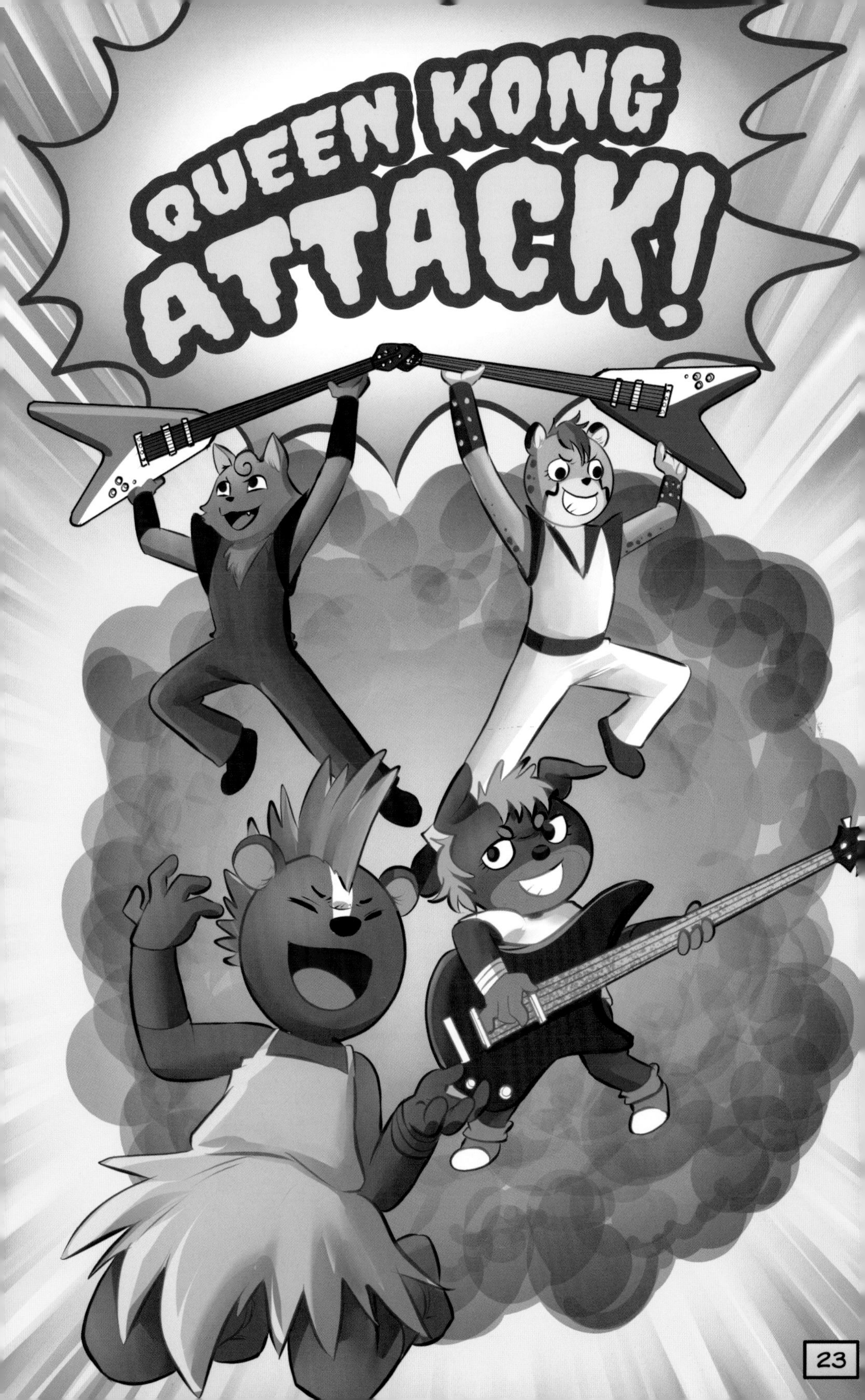
QUEEN KONG
ATTACK!

SO, YOU WANT TO PLAY WITH US IN THE BATTLE OF THE BANDS?
SURE. SOUNDS FUN!
WAIT, RORA.
YOU'RE A DETECTIVE, NOT A MUSICIAN.
WHY NOT BOTH?
MAYBE THESE BOOTS WERE MADE FOR ROCKING.
AND SOLVING MYSTERIES!

WOW!
DID YOU SEE WHAT THE WINNER OF THE CONTEST GETS?
BATTLE OF THE BANDS
A FREE LUNCH WITH FAMOUS ROCK STAR DAVID BOW-WOWIE!
FREE LUNCH?!
I SHOULD START A BAND!

BANG!
BLOP!
CRASH!
CLICK!
RETURN TO BASE
BANG!
OOPS!
CRASH!

MY BEAKERS!
MY SNACKS!
OUR FILES!

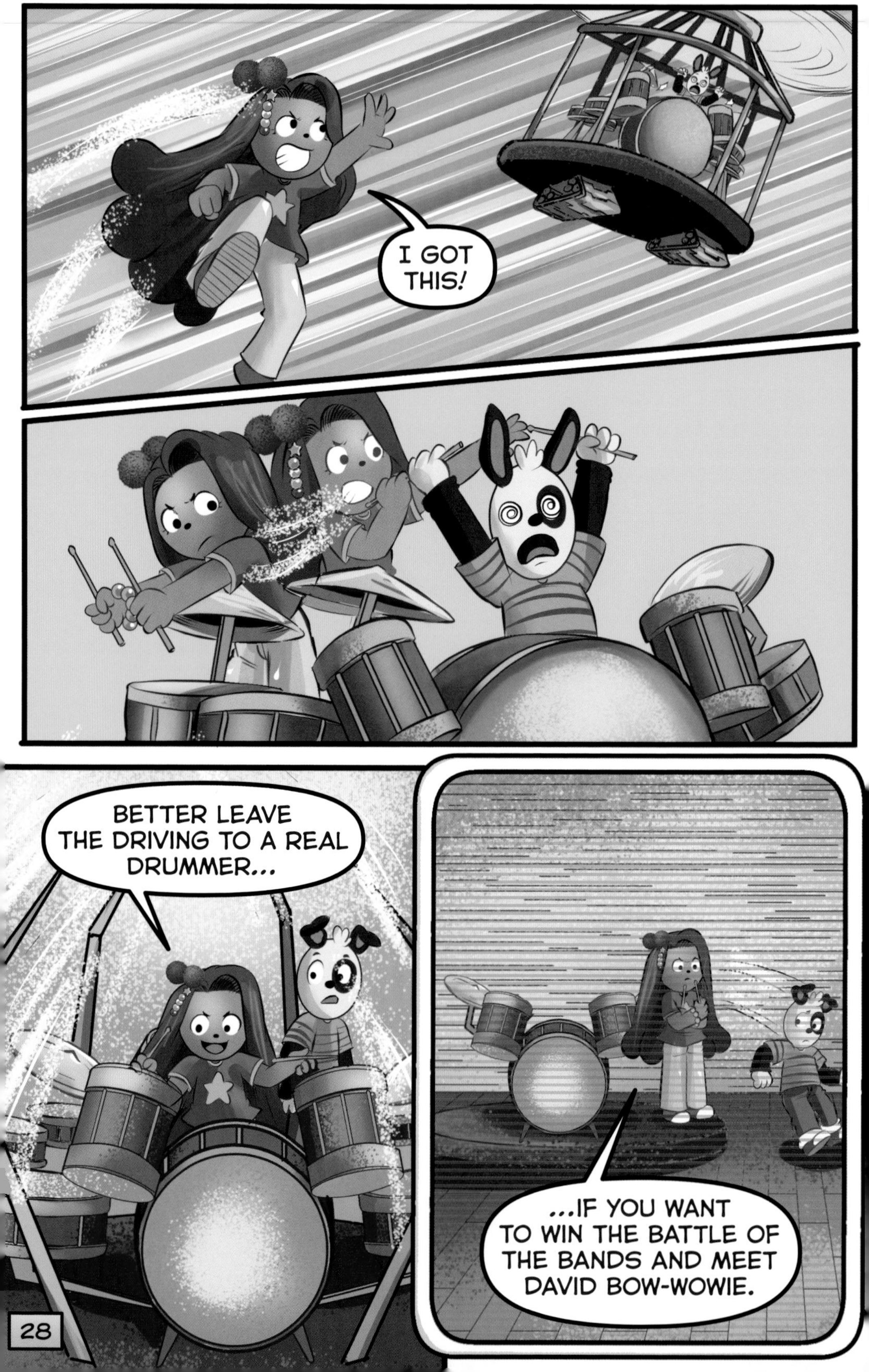

I GOT THIS!

BETTER LEAVE THE DRIVING TO A REAL DRUMMER...

...IF YOU WANT TO WIN THE BATTLE OF THE BANDS AND MEET DAVID BOW-WOWIE.

WELL, WELL.
A CHANCE TO MEET DAVID BOW-WOWIE?

IT'S TIME FOR MY MOST DIABOLICAL PLAN YET, SO I CAN WIN THAT BATTLE.

AHAHAHA!
HEY, WHY ARE THE PUP DETECTIVES ON YOUR SCREEN?

BECAUSE I'M SPYING ON THEM WITH A HIDDEN CAMERA, DUH-DOY!

YOU HID CAMERAS IN THEIR CLUBHOUSE?
SILLY FRENCHIE...
...I'VE GOT CAMERAS *EVERYWHERE*, BUT THAT'S NOT IMPORTANT.
WHAT *IS* IMPORTANT IS THAT I'VE GOT WORK TO DO IN TOWN...
...*FUNKY* WORK.
I HAD NO IDEA MATTY LIVED IN FUNKYTOWN.

CHAPTER 3

BATTLE OF THE

MOVE IT, KID!

THIS EQUIPMENT ISN'T GOING TO SET ITSELF UP!

HAVEN'T SEEN A STAGEHAND MOVE THIS SLOW SINCE I TOURED WITH SLOTH AND THE FAMILY STONE BACK IN THE DAY!

HEY! CAREFUL WITH THAT AXE, EUGENE!

THAT WAS THE BASS GUITAR THAT WAS USED ON "I WANNA HOLD YOUR PAW."

AND EASY WITH THAT MIC!

THIS IS THE MIC USED ON THE BACKUP CHORUS OF "BARK IN THE U.S.A."

AND GENTLE WITH THAT POWER STRIP, KID!

IT'S *THE* POWER STRIP DAVID BOW-WOWIE USED FOR HIS TEAPOT WHEN RECORDING "ALL THE YOUNG PUPS."

WOW!
SO MUCH ROCK HISTORY IN ONE–

WHOAAAAA!

HEADS UP!
THIS GUITAR CAN'T FLY.
IT WAS MADE TO DO ONLY ONE THING: *ROCK!*

WHAT WAS THAT?
CLICK!

SCREEECH!

DIDN'T I TELL YOU TO WATCH YOUR TAIL?
SCREEECH!

BUT I WASN'T EVEN NEAR THIS AMP.
CLICK!

BWARHHHHHHHH
THIS STAGE IS HAUNTED!
MAYBE IT'S PART OF BOW-WOWIE'S ACT.

LIKE WHEN I WAS ON TOUR WITH ALICE COUGAR...
I AM THE GHOST WITH THE MOST!
ROCK 'N' ROLL SO HOT IT WILL BURN... YOUR...TOAST!

WELL.
I STAND
CORRECTED.
IT IS A
GHOST!
HELLO?
PROFESSIONAL
LIFTERS? I NEED HELP
UNRAVELING THIS.
IT'S FUN
TO BAT THIS BALL
AROUND, BUT I CAN'T
PLAY MUSIC WITHOUT
THESE CABLES.

UMM. MATTY.
I THINK THESE STAGEHANDS MIGHT HAVE THEIR STAGE HANDS FULL.
THESE INSTRUMENTS BELONG TO ME.
WATCH ME TAKE THEM ONE TWO THREE!

HEY. NO ONE SING-YELLSSSS IN MATTY MEOW'S FACE AND GETS AWAY WITH IT.
PARDON ME, RIDER. YOU ARE IN MY WAY.
NOT SO FAST, MATTY!

CHAPTER 4
BATTLE OF THE BANDS
TIME TO GET TO THE BOTTOM OF WHO ROCKED, ROLLED, AND STOLE THESE INSTRUMENTS.

AND I KNOW JUST WHO TO TALK TO FIRST.

MATTY, I WANNA KNOW SOMETHING.

WOULD YOU LIKE SOME WARM MILK?

MAYBE A BLANKET?
HERE, PUT YOUR FEET UP.

THAT'S SSSSO THOUGHTFUL, RIDER.
I WAS FEELING STRESSED.
WHY ARE YOU BEING SO NICE TO ME?
WHY DID YOU STEAL THE INSTRUMENTS, MATTY?
TO CATCH YOU OFF GUARD!

MATTY DIDN'T DO IT.
I WAS WITH HIM.
THE GHOST WAS ONSTAGE WHEN WE GOT HERE.
DID YOU SAY A G-G-GHOST?
YOU BETTER BELIEVE IT!
THE GHOST FLOATED THE INSTRUMENTS RIGHT OUT THE DOOR, PAST RIDER.

THAT'SSSS RIGHT!
RIDER WAS THE LAST ONE TO SSSSEE THEM!

IS THAT TRUE?
KIND OF?
I HEARD SCREECHING AND CAME TO INVESTIGATE.

I WAS TOO BUSY LOOKING FOR A NEW CASE...

...THAT I MISSED THE CLUES FLYING RIGHT BY.
A LIKELY STORY, RIDER.

I KNOW!
LET'S CHECK MATTY'S SECRET CAMERAS!
THEY'RE EVERYWHERE!

SECRET *WHAT NOW?*

OH, FRENCHIE MEANS...
MY BAND: THE SECRET CAMERAS. YES!

IN FACT, I NEED TO GO PRACTICE TO WIN THE BATTLE.
WE'RE, UM, REALLY BAD RIGHT NOW.

THAT'S ONE THING WE CAN AGREE ON.
YOU *ARE* REALLY BAD.

AHH, BUT PRACTICE MAKESSSS PERFECT!

LET'S GO, FRENCHIE.

COOL...

AM I IN YOUR BAND NOW?

OKAY, BOSS.

WE WRAPPED UP THE CRIME SCENE JUST LIKE YOU ASKED.

GOOD JOB. MAYBE *TOO* GOOD.

UNWRAP THOSE STAGE HANDS WHILE RORA AND I SCARE UP MORE CLUES.

SORRY, GUYS.
HERE'S SOME MILK TO CALM YOUR NERVES.
SO... WHAT HAPPENED HERE?

I'VE NEVER SEEN ANYTHING LIKE IT.
AND I TOURED WITH THE GRATEFUL DEER, SO I'VE SEEN SOME THINGS.
THAT'S TRUE. HE AIN'T AFRAID OF NOTHING.
BUT HE LOOKED LIKE A FRIGHTENED KID WHEN THAT GHOST STARTED TALKING.
HEY!

WHAT DID THE GHOST SAY?
WAS IT *BOO*, OR A MOAN, OR JUST CHAINS JINGLING?
IT SANG A SONG THAT WENT LIKE THIS:
I'M THE GHOST WITH THE MOST!
ROCK 'N' ROLL SO HOT IT WILL BURN YOUR TOAST!
OH, THAT IS VERY SCARY.
AGREED!
RHYMING GHOST WITH MOST AND TOAST.
BLECH!

IT'S A GHOST!

IT CAN SING WHATEVER IT WANTS!

CAN YOU TELL US WHAT EXACTLY WENT MISSING?

EVERYTHING!

DAVID BOW-WOWIE WAS GONNA PLAY AT THE BATTLE OF THE BANDS AS A SURPRISE.
AND HE ONLY USES PRICELESS INSTRUMENTS.
THE FLUTE FROM "RUMBLE IN THE JUNGLE."
THE COWBELL FROM "ROCK LOBSTER."
EVEN THE TAMBOURINE FROM "DIAMOND DOGS."

POOF!

THEY'RE ALL GONE...

...AND GHOST OR NO GHOST, MR. BOW-WOWIE IS GOING TO BE SO MAD AT US!

CHAPTER 5

BIG NEWS, EVERYBODY... THE PUP DETECTIVES HAVE A MYSTERY TO SOLVE.
THE CASE OF THE MISSING MUSICAL INSTRUMENTS!

I WOULD HAVE GONE WITH GHOST RHYME CRIME, BUT YOUR TITLE WORKS.
I'LL START SCANNING THE AREA.
PEWWWWWWWW
OF THE BANDS
MY BREAK-IN-BUSTER SHOULD TELL US IF ANYONE SNUCK IN UNDER OUR NOSES.
AND...

...NOTHING!

THE DOORS WERE ALL OPEN.

THE WINDOWS WERE ALL LOCKED.

AND NO SKYLIGHT IN SIGHT FOR A THIEF TO SNEAK THROUGH.

NO SKYLIGHTS FOR THIEVES?
WELL, I'M OUT OF IDEAS, THEN.

THERE HAS TO BE SOMETHING.
RORA, WHY DON'T WE...

...GET READY TO BANG THOSE DRUMS SO WE CAN BANG SOME HEADS?

WHAT'S GOING ON IN HERE?

WE HAVE A NEW CASE.

DAVID BOW-WOWIE'S INSTRUMENTS...

YEAH, I DON'T CARE.

AS LONG AS THE BATTLE OF THE BANDS IS STILL HAPPENING.

OH. PROBABLY NOT.

WHAT?

IT'S NOT HAPPENING?

OH WHAAAT!

NOW, NOW, STUDENTS.
SETTLE DOWN.

THE PUP DETECTIVES WILL GET THOSE INSTRUMENTS BACK.

THE BATTLE OF THE BANDS WILL HAPPEN BY HOOK OR BY CROOK.

OR MY NAME ISN'T ALFRED BROCKWORST BARKLEY!

WHO?

I THOUGHT YOUR NAME WAS PRINCIPAL?

YOUR NAME *IS* PRINCIPAL. THAT MEANS THE PUP DETECTIVES *WON'T* SOLVE THE CASE!

AND THAT MEANS THE BATTLE OF THE BANDS *IS* CANCELLED!
OH NOOOOOOOOO!
RELAX, EVERYONE. WE WILL FIND THOSE INSTRUMENTS.
BECAUSE THE SHOW MUST GO ON!

IN THAT CASE, WE NEED TO PRACTICE.

COME ON, RORA.

HEY, WHAT ABOUT THE CASE?
HMM. I *DO* WANT TO SOLVE IT.

BUT I *ALSO* WANT TO ROCK!

YOU GET THIS ONE.
I'LL SOLVE THE NEXT ONE.

CAN YOU BELIEVE THIS?
I KNOW!

NOT CHASING THE GHOST WAS AN OPTION ALL THIS TIME?

DID YOU KNOW THIS, WESTIE?
I DID NOT.

I AM CHOOSING TO IGNORE BOTH OF YOU.

WESTIE, DO YOU HAVE ANY OTHER INVENTIONS THAT COULD HELP?

I HAVE ONE OR TWO THAT MIGHT JUST WORK.

MY CLOSER-UPPER IS A ROBOT ARM THAT CLOSES THINGS YOU FORGOT TO CLOSE.

UNLESS IT CAN *CLOSE* THIS CASE, NO THANKS.

BAM

BAM

BAM

MAYBE THE OPENER-UPPER ROBOT ARM WILL WORK?
IT OPENS THINGS.
WE DON'T NEED CASES *OPEN*, WESTIE.

UH-OH. THIS IS GETTING OUT OF HAND.

TIME TO USE THE WATER WAITER ARM.

YOU GOT ANY NON-ROBOT ARM INVENTIONS, WESTIE?

JUST ONE.

MY GHOST POINTERS!
THEY CAN POINT OUT WHERE GHOSTS HAVE BEEN!

BATTLE OF THE BANDS

PRINCIPAL BARKLEY!

YOU'VE BEEN A GHOST THIS WHOLE TIME?

OF COURSE NOT!

BUT THIS STYLISH TIE OF MINE IS VINTAGE.
COULD IT BE THAT?

THERE ARE NO GHOSTS HERE.
UGLY OLD TIES. NO GHOSTS!

WHICH MEANS SOMEONE *REAL* IS TRYING TO STOP THE CONTEST.

BUT WHO?
I DON'T KNOW. BUT I KNOW HOW TO FIND OUT.

IT'S TIME TO GO UNDERCOVER!

CHAPTER 6
LET'S START WITH "REBEL SQUIRREL" AND THEN GO TO–
KNOCK KNOCK KNOCK
I THINK IT'S FOR YOU, RORA.
RIDER? ZIGGY? WESTIE? WHAT ARE YOU DOING?

OH...
NOTHING.
JUST THINKING
ABOUT HOW SAD
WE ARE.
PSST,
RORA. IT'S
US.
I KNOW!
I JUST SAID
YOUR NAMES!
WHAT
ARE YOU
DOING?

IF YOU WANT TO CATCH A STRANGE AND UNUSUAL GHOST CROOK...

...YOU HAVE TO DRESS STRANGE AND UNUSUAL.
NOW, AGAIN, THERE ARE NO SUCH THINGS AS GHOSTS.

WE THINK.
BUT SOMEONE IS TRYING TO MAKE IT SEEM THAT WAY.

SO WE ARE ENTERING THE CONTEST AS...

PUDDLE OF MELTED ICE CREAM!

WHY DID YOU PICK THAT SILLY NAME?

BECAUSE NOTHING IS AS SAD AS MELTED ICE CREAM.

BUT YOU CAN'T EVEN PLAY MUSIC?

WE DON'T NEED TO!

WE JUST NEED TO *LOOK* LIKE A BAND TO GET THE DROP ON THE THIEVES.

BECAUSE WE THINK ONE OF THE BANDS COULD BE BEHIND THE CRIME.

WANT TO SNIFF AROUND WITH US?
WELL...

...I HAVE BAND PRACTICE.
GOOD THINKING, RORA!

YOU STAY AND SPY ON YOUR BAND.
WHAT? NO WAY!

THEY ARE MY FELLOW BANDMATES!

AND *WE* ARE YOUR FELLOW DETECTIVES!

PERRRRRRFECT.

RORA AND RIDER ARE FIGHTING LIKE CATS AND DOGS.
THIS GHOST CAN HELP ME SOLVE TWO PROBLEMS.
BREAK UP THE PUP DETECTIVES *AND* WIN THE BATTLE OF THE BANDS.
NOW, IF I COULD JUST FINISH UNTANGLING THESE CABLES.
FRENCHIE!

GETTING CLOSE, MATTY!
AAARGGH.
MY FEELINGS ARE STARTING TO MATCH THESE DISGUISES.
UEEN KONG ATTACK PRACTICE ROOM
CHEER UP, RIDER.
MAYBE MY INVENTIONS CAN HELP BREAK YOUR FUNK!

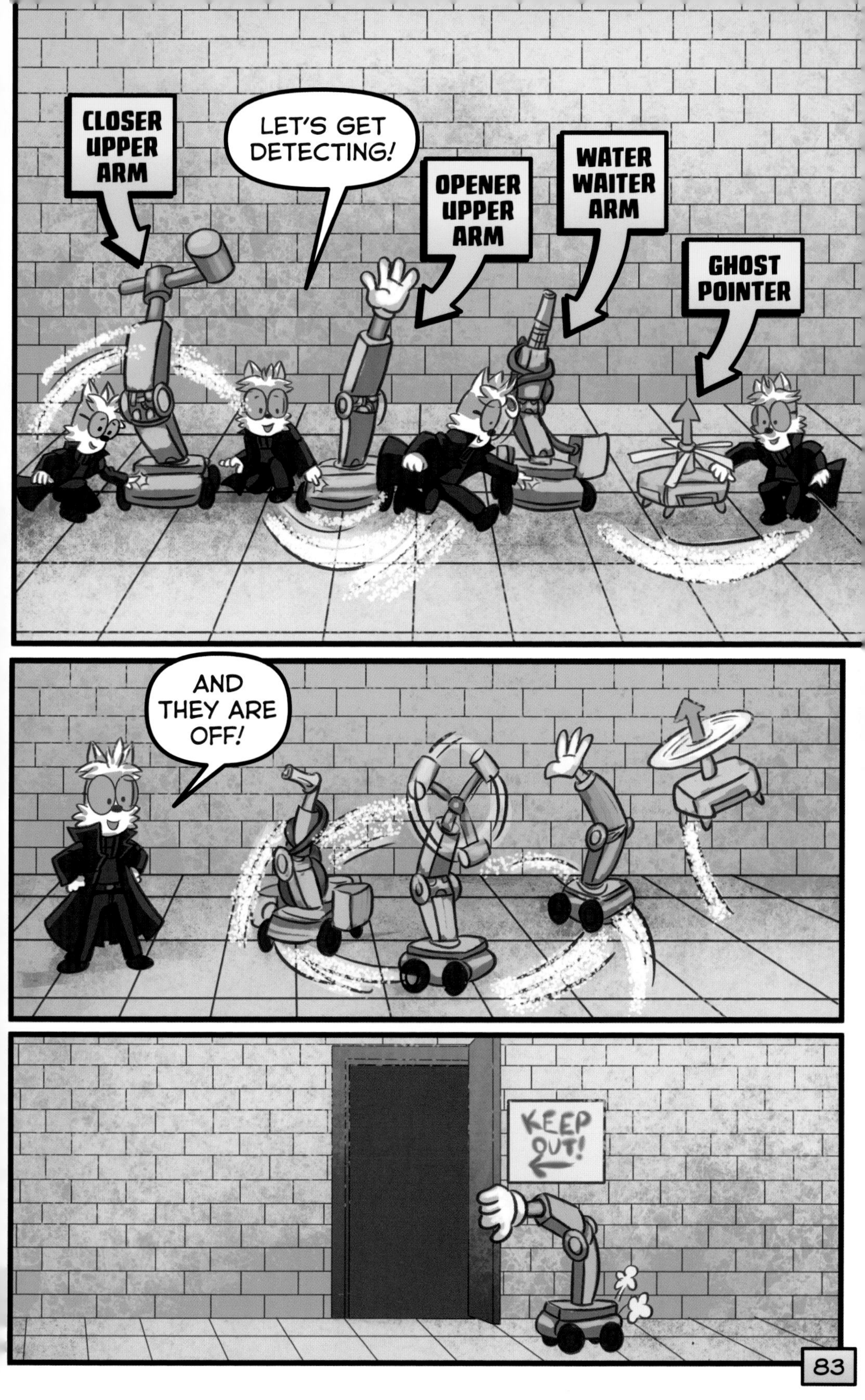
CLOSER UPPER ARM
LET'S GET DETECTING!
OPENER UPPER ARM
WATER WAITER ARM
GHOST POINTER
AND THEY ARE OFF!
KEEP OUT!

HEY! WE ARE TRYING TO PRACTICE HERE–

DISCLAW

NOT TAKE A BATH.

NOPE. THEY ARE CLEAN.

DOGBOLE

IT'S DOGBOLE, THE DJ WHO ALWAYS WEARS A MASK. I WONDER WHAT THEY LOOK LIKE IN REAL LIFE.

WHAT'S GOING ON!

NOT COOL!

SURPRISING, BUT NO MISSING INSTRUMENTS HERE.

Red Lion

OH NOOOO!!!

HEY!

GUINEA PIG EAT WORLD

UGGH. YOU ARE MAKING US SOUND LIKE THEM!

AND WE SOUND LIKE THEM.

NO GOOOOOD!

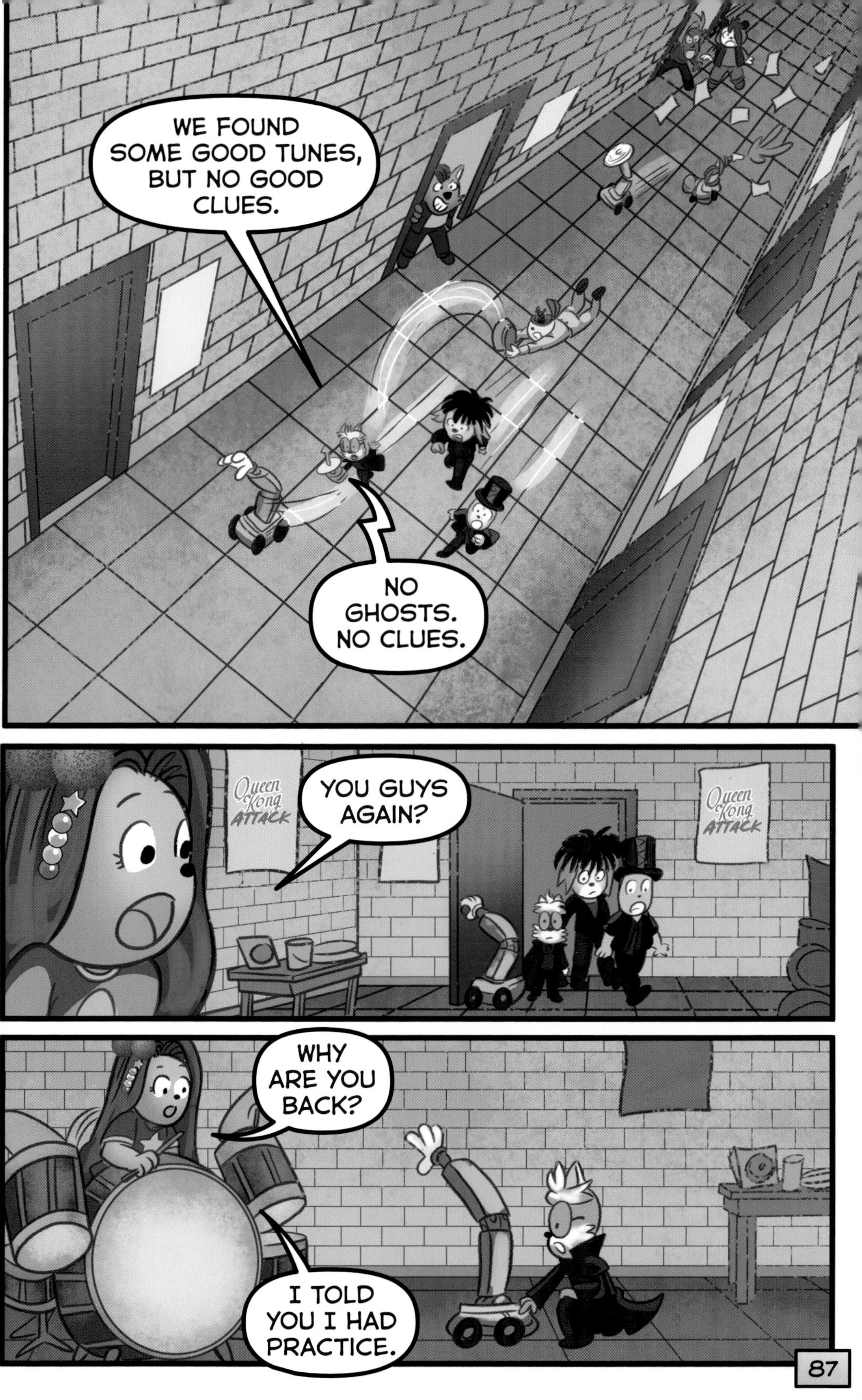

WE FOUND SOME GOOD TUNES, BUT NO GOOD CLUES.

NO GHOSTS. NO CLUES.

SORRY. STILL LOOKING FOR THE CULPRIT.
AND LUNCH.

YA GOT ANY?
NO!

ALRIGHT. FROM THE TOP.
HEY, THAT TAMBOURINE IS EXACTLY LIKE THE ONE WE'RE LOOKING FOR.

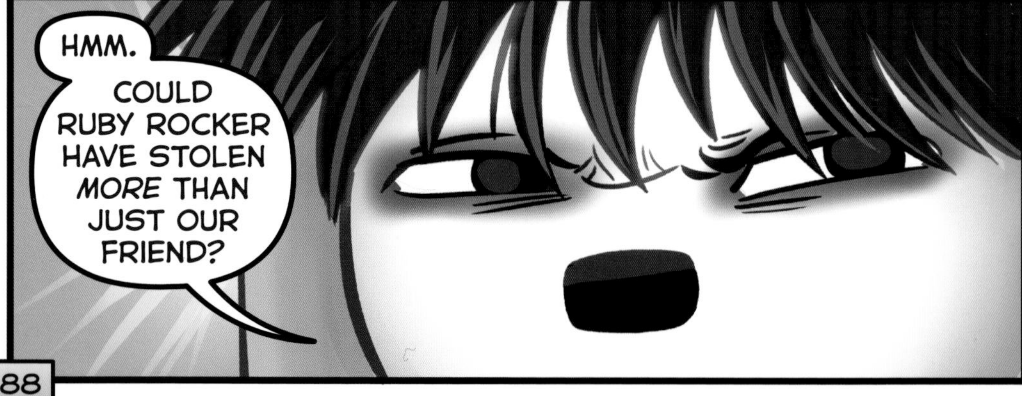
HMM.
COULD RUBY ROCKER HAVE STOLEN *MORE* THAN JUST OUR FRIEND?

CHAPTER 7

BATTLE OF THE BANDS
WOW, PACKED HOUSE OUT THERE.
PACKED HOUSE.
WOW.
YEAH, YOU SAID THAT ALREADY.
RIDER, ARE YOU NERVOUS?

NO, NO. I JUST WANT TO FIND THOSE MISSING INSTRUMENTS...

BEFORE WE HAVE TO PLAY ANY INSTRUMENTS.

HEY, RORA!

OH, HELLO, RORA.
I SEE YOU STILL PLAN ON PLAYING.

I SUPPOSE SO.
THEN I SUPPOSE I'LL SAY GOOD LUCK.

AND I SUPPOSE I'LL SAY WE DON'T NEED IT.
I SUPPOSE NOT.

BESIDES, I ALREADY SOLVED THE CASE.
REALLY? WHO DID IT?

YOUR SINGER, RUBY!
WHAT? NO WAY!
YOU'RE JUST JEALOUS.

WHAT?
JEALOUS I FOUND A NEW FRIEND *AND* A NEW HOBBY.

HOW DARE YOU.
DETECTING IS NOT A HOBBY!

IT'S A WAY OF LIFE!
WELL, WHATEVER IT IS.

I THINK YOUR JEALOUSY KEPT YOU FROM SEEING A POSSIBLE SUSPECT.

ROTTEN RUFFHOUSE!

WHAT IS ROTTEN DOING HERE?

HE HATES HEALTHY COMPETITION.
EXACTLY WHAT I WAS THINKING!

HMM.
CRIMINALS OFTEN RETURN TO THE SCENE OF THE CRIME.
I DON'T KNOW, YOU GUYS.

COULD YOUR FEELINGS BE GETTING IN THE WAY OF SOLID DETECTIVE WORK?

ZIGGY'S RIGHT.
SURE, SOMETIMES ROTTEN IS UP TO NO GOOD.

BUT LET'S NOT POINT FINGERS WITHOUT PROOF.

OH, ROTTEN WILL SLIP UP.

THEN YOU'LL SEE RUBY ROCKER IS INNOCENT.

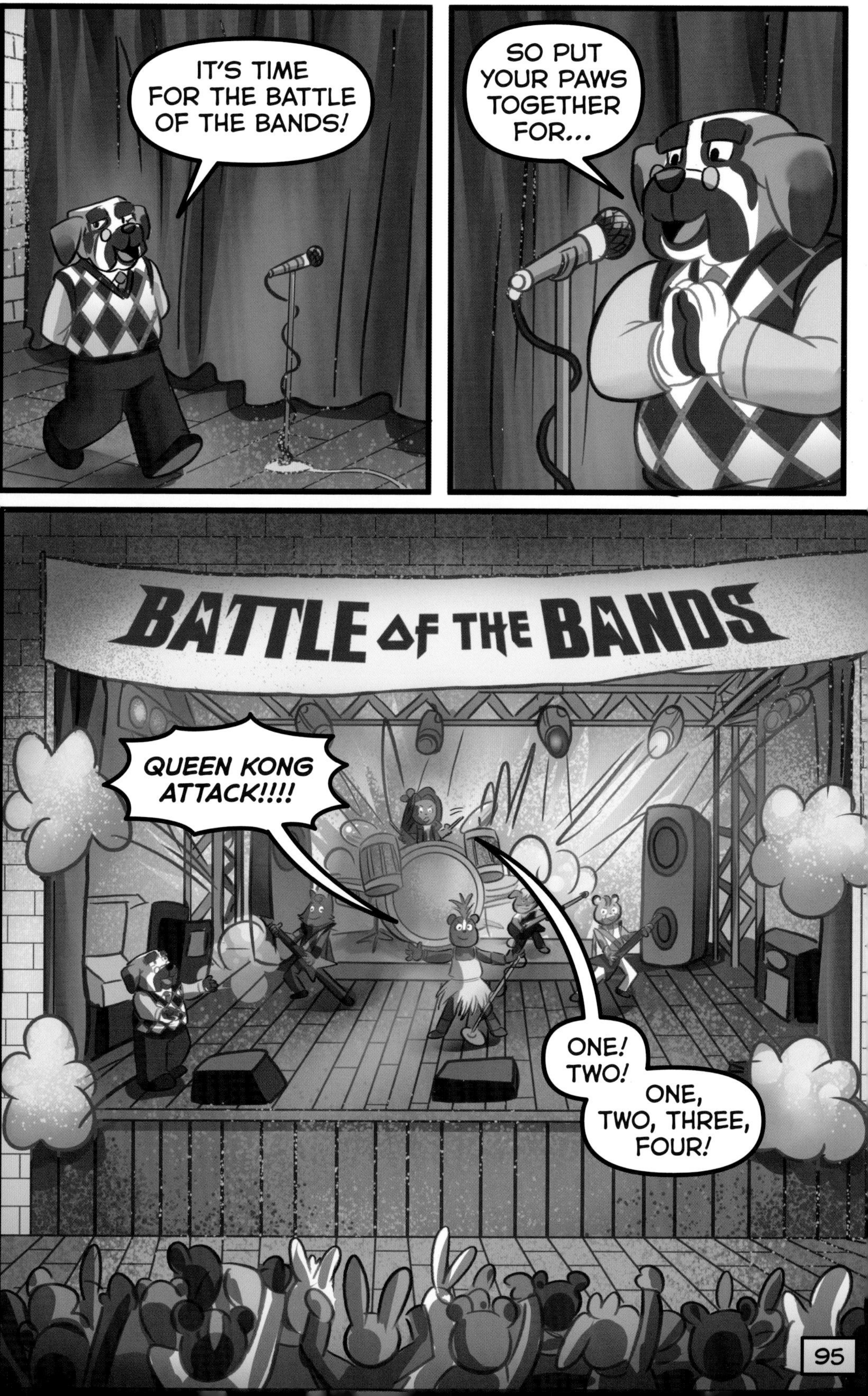

BATTLE OF THE BANDS

QUEEN KONG ATTACK!!!!

ONE! TWO!

ONE, TWO, THREE, FOUR!

REBEL SQUIRREL!
REBEL SQUIRREL!
YOU ARE THE QUEEN OF MY SQUIRREL!

HMMM.
MAYBE RORA AND I WERE *BOTH* WRONG.

MAYBE ROTTEN AND RUBY JUST LIKE TO ROCK.

SPOKE TOO SOON, I GUESS.

TIME TO MAKE THESE DRUMS FLY.

GREAT DRUMMING, RORA!
NOW LET'S CATCH THAT DOG!

CHAPTER 8

HEY!
THAT'S THE ONLY DRUM SET!
NOT COOL!!!
NO BANDS LEFT? THEN IT'S DJ MEOWLIX TIME!

OH NO.
RIDER AND HIS CREW ARE ON MY CASE AGAIN.
I'M OUT OF HERE!
OKAY, PUP DETECTIVES.
TIME TO REMEMBER WHAT IT'S LIKE TO WORK TOGETHER AGAIN!

WESTIE, HOW DO I STEER THIS THING?
IT'S EASY!
THE DRUMS WILL TURN WHERE YOU HIT THEM.
JUST WATCH OUT FOR THE DANCERS AT THE DANCE-A-THON.
DANCE -A- THON

OOPS. SORRY. GETTING THE HANG OF IT.
HOPE I DIDN'T BREAK THAT BREAK DANCE.
SORRY TO RUIN YOUR FUN.
GIVE IT HERE, WESTIE.
LET ME TRY.

OOPS. THIS LOOKS BAD ALREADY.
SORRY.
OUCH.
TIME TO GIVE SOMEONE ELSE A SHOT.
HOW ABOUT WE LET THE REAL MUSICIAN DRIVE?

THANKS, RIDER.
THANK ME BY CATCHING ROTTEN.
I SURRENDER! YOU GOT ME!
BUT WHAT DID I DO?

YOU STOLE RUBY'S TAMBOURINE!
NOT TO MENTION DAVID BOW-WOWIE'S INSTRUMENTS!

WELL, THIS ISN'T EVEN RUBY'S!

SEE, IT BELONGS TO DAVID BOW-WOWIE.
OFFICIAL DAVID BOW-WOWIE REPLICA
REPLICA?

OH NO! WHAT'S A REPLICA?

IS IT A GHOST? A GOBLIN? A GHOST GOBLIN?

NO, ZIGGY.
REPLICA JUST MEANS IT IS A COPY.

THIS ISN'T THE STOLEN TAMBOURINE.
WOW. RORA. I'M SORRY.

I WAS WRONG TO BLAME RUBY.
AND I'M SORRY.
I SHOULD HAVE KNOWN LETTING THE AUDIENCE TAKE THE TAMBOURINE WAS PART OF HER ACT.

WHERE'S MY APOLOGY?
I DIDN'T DO NOTHING.
NOT THIS TIME.

CAN WE TAKE A RAIN CHECK FOR THE NEXT ROTTEN THING YOU DO?
YEAH. SOUNDS FAIR.

BUT YOU DID RUIN MY DAY!
OH NO. WE RUINED EVERYONE'S DAY!

WE TOOK THE ONLY DRUM SET AT THE BATTLE OF THE BANDS.

LET'S GET THESE BEATS BACK!

CHAPTER 9
WHAT IS THAT AWFUL SOUND?
PAWSTON ELEMENTERY SCHOOL
AS A BIG MUSIC FAN, I CAN SAY, THAT IS *NOT* MUSIC!

OH NO! IS THE GHOST BACK?
DID IT STEAL ALL THE GOOD MUSIC IN THE WORLD?
THIS IS *HORRIBLY* HAUNTED.
NO. THIS IS MATTY.

SCRATCH
SCRATCH
WHAT'S UP, PAWSTON!
DJ MEOWLIX ON THE ONES AND TWOS.
WITH NO OTHER BANDS PLAYING, I CAN'T LOSE.
SCRATCH
SCRATCH
THEY ARE EATING THIS UP.
SCRATCH
SCRATCH

NOW WHO WANTS KIBBLE CAKE?!
WHY IS HE THROWING KIBBLE CAKE ON THE AUDIENCE?
DON'T WORRY. I'LL TAKE CARE OF IT.

MATTY'S STAGE SHOW IS JUST AS CONFUSING AS HIS MUSIC.

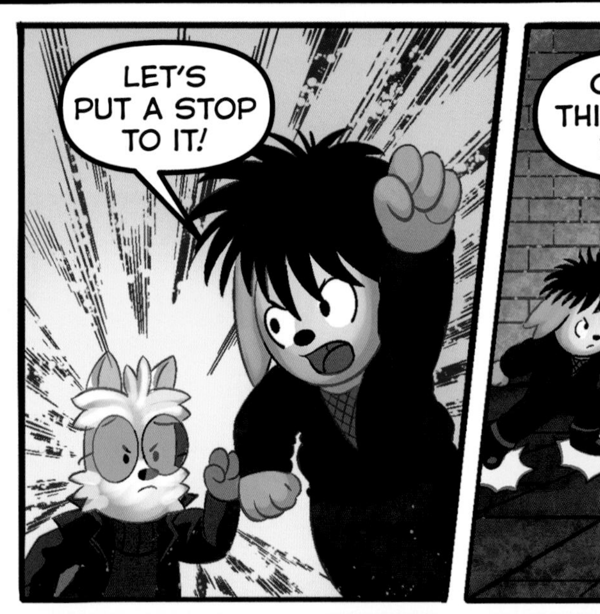
LET'S PUT A STOP TO IT!

CHECK OUT THIS SICK BEAT, PAWSTON.

HEY!

YOU NEED TO TAKE THAT SICK BEAT TO THE DOCTOR!

YAYYYYY!!!!

RIDER, LOOK! A FLOATING GUITAR!

WHAAAAAA?

IT'S THE STOLEN INSTRUMENTS.
THEY'RE RETURNING THEMSELVES?
I'VE HEARD OF AIR GUITAR...
...BUT THIS IS RIDICULOUS!

LET'S CATCH THIS "GHOST" ONCE AND FOR ALL.

YEAHHH!!

WOW!

MUSIC REALLY ***DOES*** BRING PEOPLE TOGETHER.

LET'S GO!!!
WHOOSH
CRASH

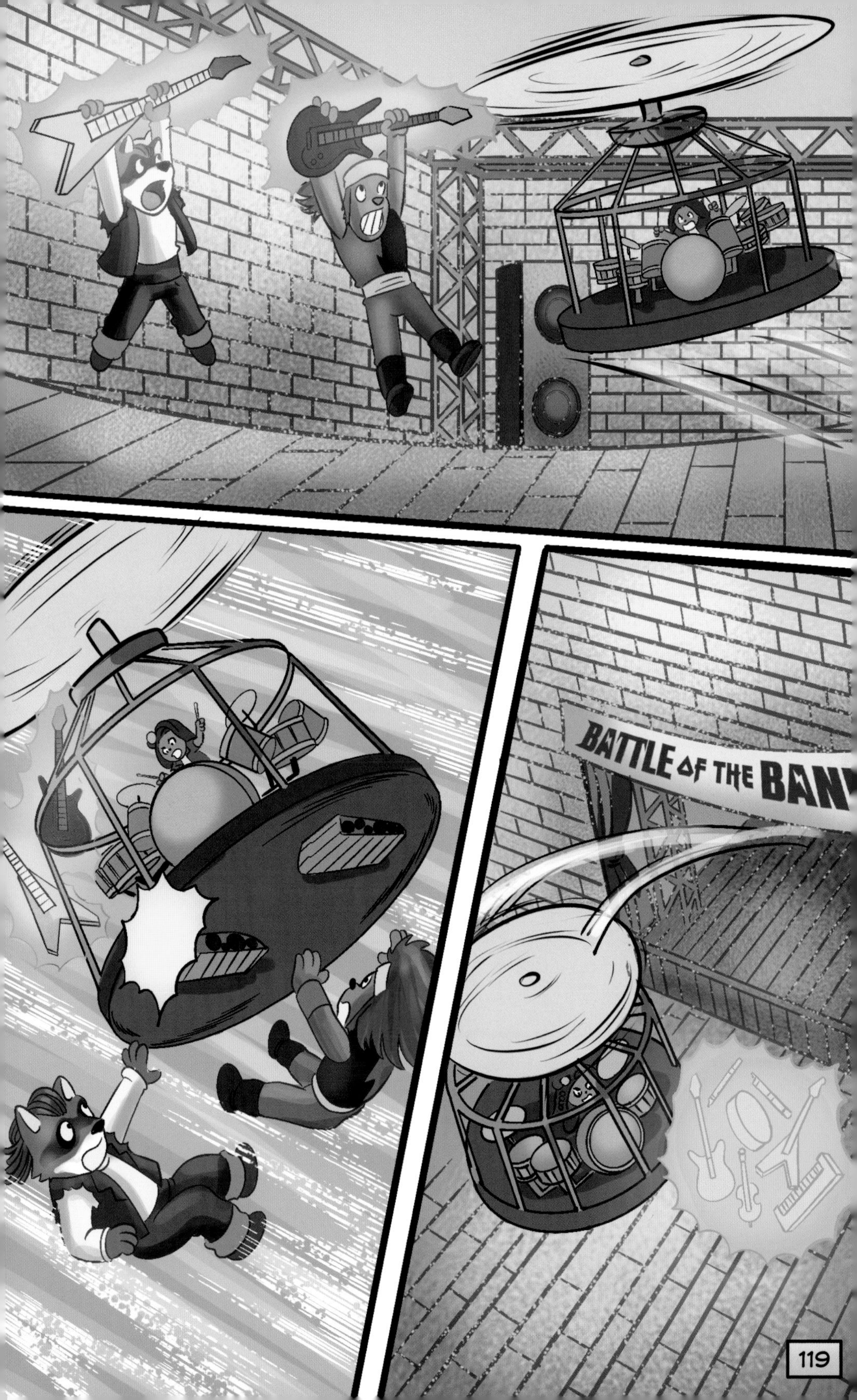
BATTLE OF THE BAN

LET'S ROUND THEM UP, EVERYONE.
CIRCLE PIT!

DAVID BOW-WOWIE!

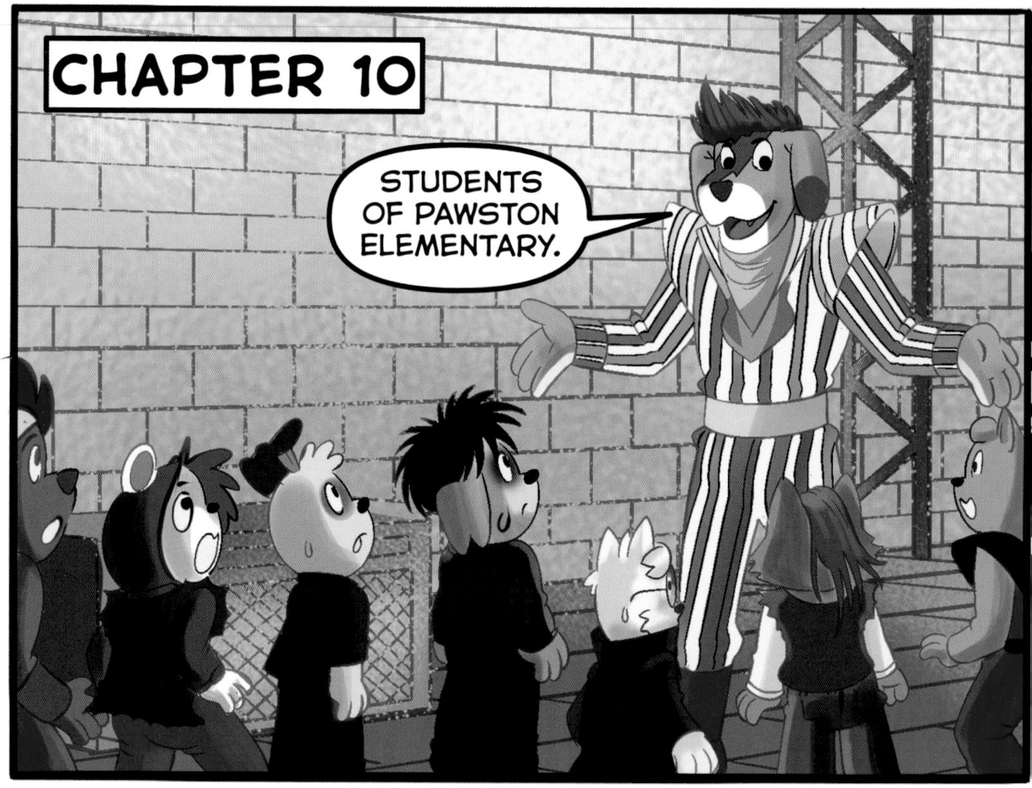

CHAPTER 10

STUDENTS OF PAWSTON ELEMENTARY.

I'M AFRAID I OWE YOU ALL AN APOLOGY!

WHAT YOU WITNESSED...

...WAS NOT A GHOST.
OH NO!

IT WAS, IN FACT...

...THE NEXT STAGE OF ROCK 'N' ROLL.

YOU SEE, I'M ALWAYS LOOKING FOR THE NEWEST WAY TO ROCK.

AND I THOUGHT, WHAT IF YOU HAD A BAND...

...THAT WASN'T A BAND?

I PRESENT TO YOU MY NEWEST BACKING BAND...

DAVID BOW-
WOWIE AND THE
GHOST ANTS FROM
MARS!

BRING DOWN THE MAGNIFYING GLASS.
THIS IS A NEW SPECIES OF FLOATING ANTS.

GHOST ANTS! INVISIBLE TO THE NAKED EYE.
AND F-*ANT*-ASTIC MUSICIANS!

SO SORRY IF I SCARED ANYONE.
PERHAPS I COULD MAKE IT UP WITH A SONG?
YEAHHHHHHH!
THIS IS A NEW ONE CALLED "GHOST TOAST!"

ONE, TWO, THREE, FOUR!
I AM THE GHOST WITH THE MOST.
ROCK 'N' ROLL SO HOT IT WILL BURN YOUR TOAST!

GHOST TOAST!

WOW, I AM LOVING THIS SONG!

WHAT WAS THAT? DIDN'T QUITE HEAR YOU.

TOO BUSY ROCKING OUT TO THESE AWESOME LYRICS.

HEY, BANDS.

WHY DON'T YOU GET UP HERE AND JOIN ME!

LET'S ROCK TOGETHER!

GHOST TOAST!

GHOST TOAST!

WELL, THIS IS A DREAM COME TRUE.
JUST WAIT UNTIL DAVID HEARS MY GROOVES.
WE'RE GONNA BE BEST FRIENDS!

DAVID! CHECK THIS OUT!
SCREECH!
SCRATCH!

HOLD UP.

SORRY, LAD.

MAYBE YOU SHOULD JUST CLAP...
QUIETLY... FAR AWAY FROM THE STAGE.

QUEEN KONG ATTACK! WHERE ARE YOU?

I HEARD YOU PLAY BEFORE THE CONTEST STOPPED.
QUITE GOOD.
JOIN ME ON THIS NEXT VERSE!
YOU TOO, PUP DETECTIVES!

WHAT DO YOU SAY?
I SUPPOSE DETECTING IS KIND OF COOL.
NOT AS COOL AS ROCKING!
ALRIGHT!

SOMETIMES THE GREATEST CRIME IS... NO CRIME AT ALL.
JUST SOME CROSSED WIRES. LUCKILY, TODAY EVERYONE TURNED OUT TO BE A WINNER.

MATTY, I ALMOST GOT THE WIRES UNTANGLED.
WELL, ALMOST EVERYONE. SORRY, MATTY.

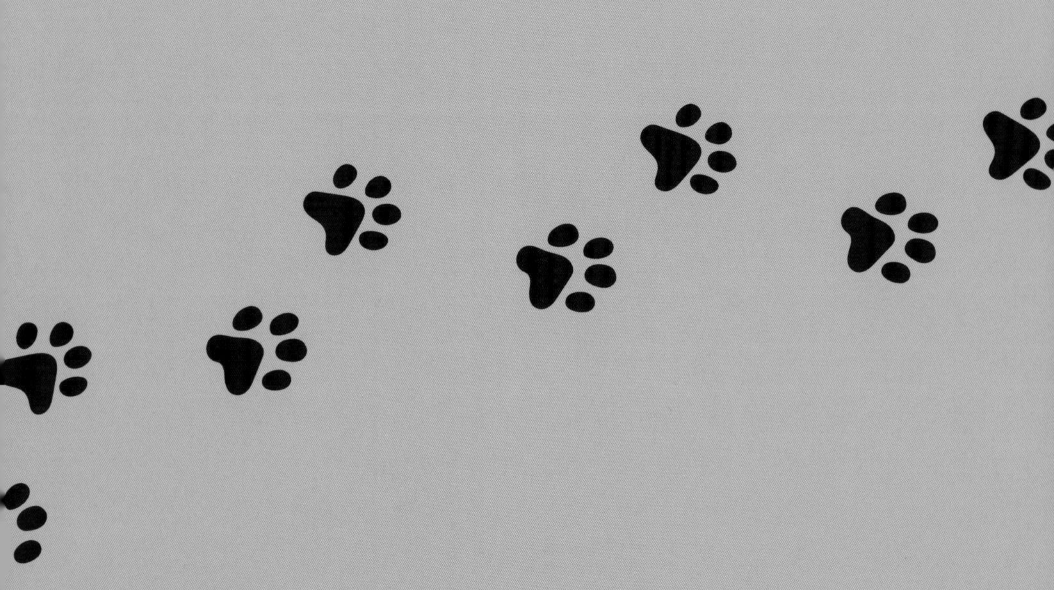

WHAT?
DID YOU THINK I
WOULD BE BEHIND
THIS ONE? GUESS
AGAIN!

DON'T YOU DARE FORGET ABOUT THESE **ADVENTURES** TOO!

Graphic Novel
PUP DETECTIVES
FEATURING...
THE TIGER'S EYE
WESTIE BARKER
ZIGGY FLUFFENSTUFF
MATTY MEOW

Graphic Novel
PUP DETECTIVES
FEATURING...
THE FIRST CASE
RORA GOODDOG
WESTIE BARKER
?
PAWSTON ELEMENTARY · P.I. Pack · #001
1

Graphic Novel
PUP DETECTIVES
FEATURING...
THE SOCCER MYSTERY
MATTY MEOW
ROTTEN RUFFHOUSE
DAVID GECKOM
P.I. Pack · #003
3

Graphic Novel!
PUP DETECTIVES
FEATURING...
GHOSTS, GOBLINS, AND NINJAS!
SENSEI
GOBLIN
NINJAS
PAWSTON ELEMENTARY
P.I. PACK
#004
4

Graphic Novel!
PUP DETECTIVES
FEATURING...
THE MISSING MAGIC WAND
ZIGGY
FRENCHIE
MATTY MEOW
PAWSTON ELEMENTARY
5

Graphic Novel!
PUP DETECTIVES
FEATURING...
MYSTERY MOUNTAIN GETAWAY
PRINCIPAL
POPPA
RODERICK
PAWSTON ELEMENTARY
P.I. PACK
#006
6

Graphic Novel!
PUP DETECTIVES
FEATURING...
THE BIG BAD WOOF
VICKY CROWN
BIG AL
MARTIN
7